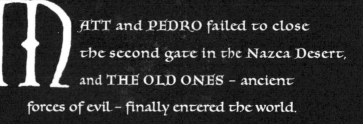**M**ATT and PEDRO failed to close
the second gate in the Nazca Desert,
and THE OLD ONES – ancient
forces of evil – finally entered the world.

Having lost the battle, Matt learnt that his only
hope was to find the three other Gatekeepers, two boys
and a girl. By coming together, they would finally
have the strength to defeat the Old Ones – and save
the world from chaos and destruction.

But the Old Ones know THE POWER OF THE FIVE
and their servants are already searching
for them, determined to keep them apart.

There are THREE WORLDS – the world now,
the world as it was before the Dark Ages, and
a STRANGE DREAM WORLD that connects the two...

SECOND SHOW.

FOR AS LONG AS I CAN REMEMBER, WE'VE KNOWN WHAT'S GOING ON INSIDE EACH OTHER'S HEADS.

IT DOESN'T MAKE IT EASY WHEN PICKING UP GIRLS.

NOW I—

I ... UM ... I NEED SOMEON TO HELP ME ON THE STAGE—

I'LL H YO

I'D LIKE YOU TO EXAMINE THE BLINDFOLD—

HOW DID YOU **DO** IT?

CAN YOU READ EACH OTHER'S MINDS?

HOW DID YOU DO THAT TRICK WITH THE NEWSPAPER?

I'D LIKE SOMETHING FROM YOUR HANDBAG—

I DON'T HAVE A HANDBAG—

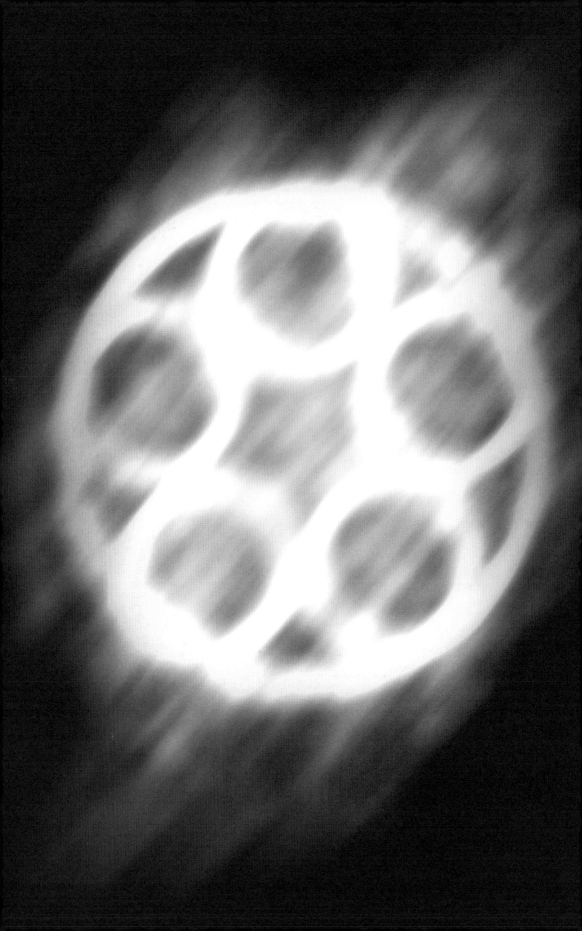

ANTHONY HOROWITZ

THE POWER OF FIVE: BOOK THREE

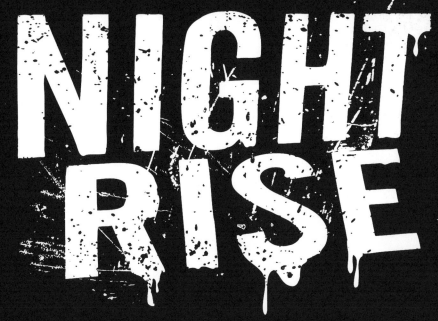

NIGHT RISE

THE GRAPHIC NOVEL

adapted by **TONY LEE**

illustrated by

NIGEL DOBBYN

WALKER

GOODNIGHT, KIDS.

GOODNIGHT, FRANK.

WHAT HAPPENED? WHAT DID YOU SEE OUT ON STAGE?

YOU SAID YOU SAW SOMEONE CALLED DANIEL — YOU SAID HE WAS BEING HURT?

I DON'T KNOW. I DON'T WANT TO TALK ABOUT IT, OK?

SORRY. I DIDN'T MEAN TO YELL AT YOU.

SOMETHING'S HAPPENING. I DON'T KNOW WHAT IT IS, BUT SOMETHING'S WRONG.

TONIGHT. THAT WOMAN. EVERYTHING. I'VE GOT A BAD FEELING.

MAYBE YOU'RE GOING TO HAVE TO LOOK OUT FOR YOURSELF—

BARK! BARK

THAT'S JAGGER!

STAY THERE — I'LL SEE WHAT'S HAPPENING —

GRRRRRRRRRRR

GRROWWLLL!!!

PHUT! PHUT!

JAMIE!!! RUN!!!

-hhff-

...MY HEAD.

YOU'RE UP — WHEN DID YOU WAKE?

IT'S AFTER TEN. I WAS GETTING WORRIED.

WHO *ARE* YOU? HOW LONG HAVE I BEEN HERE?

ARE YOU *SCOTT* OR *JAMIE*? THE TWO OF YOU ARE SO ALIKE.

I'M JAMIE.

YOU'RE IN A MOTEL. WE'RE STILL IN RENO. I THOUGHT YOU MIGHT BE HUNGRY SO I WENT SHOPPING.

YOU WERE IN THE THEATRE. THE WOMAN WITH THE *PHOTOGRAPH*.

YEAH. ACTUALLY, I'VE SEEN YOU *THREE* TIMES. I WANTED TO SEE HOW YOU DID IT. YOUR ACT.

WHERE ARE YOU GOING? YOU CAN'T JUST *WALK OUT* OF HERE — IT'S TOO LATE. IF IT WASN'T FOR ME, THEY'D HAVE TAKEN YOU TOO.

I DUG *THIS* OUT OF YOUR SHOULDER. GOD KNOWS WHAT WAS IN IT BUT YOU'VE BEEN ASLEEP FOR *ELEVEN HOURS*.

I KNOW YOU WANT TO LOOK FOR YOUR BROTHER — BUT HE WAS HIT TOO — AND NOW HE COULD BE *ANYWHERE*.

NIGHTRISE HEAD OFFICE, THE NAIL, HONG KONG.

THEY'RE COMING ONLINE *NOW*, MISTER CHAIRMAN.

GREETINGS TO YOU, LADIES AND GENTLEMEN. I DON'T NEED TO REMIND YOU THAT THIS IS A CRITICAL TIME FOR US ALL.

EVERYTHING WE HAVE BEEN WORKING FOR ALL THESE YEARS IS ABOUT TO COME TO FRUITION.

THERE IS MUCH *MORE* AT STAKE THAN SIMPLE *PROFIT* AND *LOSS*. WE HAVE THE *PSI PROJECT*. NEWS FROM SOUTH AMERICA. AND OF COURSE THE UPCOMING ELECTION –

– THE RACE TO BECOME THE MOST POWERFUL MAN IN THE WORLD. THIS IS ONE TIME THAT WE *CANNOT AFFORD* TO MAKE MISTAKES.

LET'S START IN *NEW YORK*. WHAT'S TO REPORT?

THIS IS A HARD NUT TO CRACK, SIR. OUR GUY IS DOING BETTER THAN EXPECTED, BUT WE HAVEN'T BEEN ABLE TO DO *SERIOUS* DAMAGE TO TRELAWNEY.

WE'VE TRIED *EVERYTHING* – BUT PEOPLE SEEM TO *LIKE* HIM. INDICATIONS ARE THAT IT WILL BE NECK AND NECK COME NOVEMBER.

BAKER *MUST* WIN. THERE CAN BE NO OTHER RESULT. TRELAWNEY MUST NOT BECOME PRESIDENT.

WELL... SHORT OF *ASSASSINATING* JOHN TRELAWNEY...

I THINK, MISTER SIMMS, THAT YOU SHOULD BE CONSIDERING *EVERY* POSSIBILITY.

EXIT

VOTE CHARLES BAKER

RINGG!

HELLO?

IS THIS COLTON BANES?

4925 Colton Banes

YES. WHO IS THIS?

WHO ARE YOU? WHAT ARE YOU DOING THERE?

I THINK YOU'D BETTER COME WITH ME.

WHERE IS SCOTT TYLER?

I... I DON'T...

MADE YOU THINK IT.

GOTCHA!

THE CARLTON HOTEL. WILTSHIRE BOULEVARD.

SILENT CREEK.

YOU *POOR BOY* — WHAT HAVE THEY *DONE* TO YOU? I WOULD HAVE COME SOONER, BUT IT'S DIFFICULT.

I WANT TO BE YOUR *FRIEND*.

BUT I HAVE TO KNOW YOU *TRUST* ME. YOU HAVE TO BE ON MY *SIDE*.

JAMIE *LEFT* YOU. DO YOU REMEMBER? ALL YOUR LIFE YOU LOOKED AFTER HIM AND HE DIDN'T CARE.

FIRST CHANCE HE GOT HE WAS *AWAY*, LEAVING YOU TO THIS. RIGHT NOW HE'S ALL RIGHT — AND HE'S *LAUGHING* AT YOU. HE'S HAVING A FINE OLD TIME —

— AND YOU'RE *HERE*, CONNECTED TO TUBES. YOU COULD *DIE* AND NOBODY WOULD THINK TWICE.

THE LITTLE PEOPLE WHO GET PUSHED AROUND. DO YOU WANT TO BE A *LITTLE* PERSON, SCOTT?

OR DO YOU WANT TO BE WITH *ME*? IN THIS NEW WORLD, I'M GOING TO BE IN CHARGE.

WHICH END OF THE WHIP WOULD YOU LIKE TO BE?

THINK ABOUT IT, MY DEAR. JAMIE ISN'T SENSIBLE ENOUGH TO *MAKE* THAT CHOICE. MAYBE ONE DAY YOU'LL GET YOUR OWN BACK ON HIM.

MAYBE ONE DAY WE'LL LET YOU PUT A *KNIFE* IN HIS HEART.

"I'LL LEAVE YOU BOTH *ALONE* NOW."

RIGHT NOW, I MUST GO. MAYBE TOMORROW WE'LL HAVE ANOTHER CHAT.

MISTER BANES IS HERE TO SEE YOU NOW.

I *WISH* I COULD STAY AND KEEP HIM AWAY. BUT UNTIL YOU'RE MINE, I CAN'T. BUT I WILL COME BACK, I PROMISE.

IN THE CASE OF **JEREMY RABB**, THE SENTENCE SET DOWN BY THIS COURT IS TWELVE MONTHS IN A DETENTION FACILITY.

LOOKING THROUGH THE CASE FILES I THINK **SUMMIT VIEW** WOULD BE APPROPRIATE.

WITH RESPECT, YOUR HONOUR — I WAS GOING TO RECOMMEND **SILENT CREEK**.

IT'S PRETTY TOUGH OUT THERE. THE BOY IS ONLY FOURTEEN AND THIS IS A FIRST OFFENCE.

RABB SOLD CRYSTAL METH TO KIDS AS YOUNG AS **TWELVE**. SOME OF THEM ARE IN REHAB PROGRAMMES, OUT OF SCHOOL.

RABB HAS SHOWN **NO** REMORSE — IN FACT, HE'S BEEN QUITE **PLEASED** WITH HIMSELF.

VERY WELL. IT'S A **HARD** LESSON — BUT MAYBE THAT'S WHAT HE NEEDS.

"TWELVE MONTHS AT **SILENT CREEK**."

MISTER RABB – TURN OFF THE SHOWER.

WHERE DID YOU GET THAT *TATTOO*?

I'VE *ALWAYS* HAD IT. IT WAS DONE WHEN I WAS BORN.

YOU HAVE A *BROTHER*?

NO. I *DON'T* HAVE A BROTHER.

PUT THESE ON.

I'LL TAKE YOU IN.

GREAT. I'M *HERE* AGAIN.

MAYBE THOSE TWO BOYS IN THE BOAT CAN TELL ME HOW TO FIND SCOTT?

HE'S GONNA *KILL* HIM.

THAT'S WHAT YOU SAID *LAST* TIME!

BUT I CAN'T STOP THEM KILLING SCOTT UNLESS *YOU* TELL ME WHERE HE IS!

NO, BOY. YOU DON'T *UNDERSTAND* —

NIGHTRISE HEADQUARTERS – HONG KONG.

NO. OLD ONES? WHAT ARE THEY?

THESE TWO BOYS — THEY'RE **BOTH** AT SILENT CREEK?

JAMIE'S THERE — PROBABLY. HE WAS SENT SEVERAL DAYS AGO. HE WAS GOING TO FIND OUT ABOUT HIS BROTHER WHEN HE WAS THERE.

LISTEN TO ME — YOU CAME TO ME FOR ADVICE AS AN OLD FRIEND BUT — DONT DENY IT — **ALSO** BECAUSE I'M A MEMBER OF—

THE **NEXUS.** I'VE HEARD THE NAME, ALWAYS SUSPECTED IT MIGHT HAVE SOMETHING TO DO WITH YOU.

YOU'VE BEEN TOUCHED BY SOMETHING YOU KNOW **NOTHING** ABOUT. SOMETHING **I'VE** BEEN INVOLVED IN FOR HALF MY LIFE.

SO YOU MUST **BELIEVE** ME WHEN I SAY IT IS VITAL THAT WE FIND JAMIE TYLER AND GET HIM OUT OF SILENT CREEK **IMMEDIATELY.** AND HIS BROTHER TOO IF HE'S STILL THERE.

THAT MAY NOT BE TOO EASY.

JOHN — YOU COULD BE THE NEXT PRESIDENT OF THIS COUNTRY.

BUT THERE MIGHT NOT EVEN **BE** A COUNTRY TO BE PRESIDENT OF IF YOU **DON'T** DO AS I SAY.

WHAT ARE YOU **TALKING** ABOUT? WHO ARE THESE TWO BOYS?

NOW. **THIS** IS WHAT YOU HAVE TO DO...

WHEN I ARRIVED YOU ASKED IF I HAD A *BROTHER*. HAVE YOU SEEN HIM?

I *KNEW* YOU WERE LYING TO ME. AND KORING TOLD ME YOUR *REAL* NAME.

YOU HAVE A TWIN – *SCOTT* TYLER – HE WAS SENT TO THE BLOCK. ON THE OTHER SIDE OF THE WALL.

IT WAS BECAUSE OF THE *TATTOO* THAT I KNEW WHO YOU WERE. THERE IS MUCH TO EXPLAIN TO YOU.

BUT LATER TONIGHT WHEN IT IS DARK YOU WILL LEAVE–

I'M NOT LEAVING WITHOUT SCOTT!

HE'S *GONE*. THEY TOOK HIM AWAY BEFORE YOU ARRIVED.

I DON'T KNOW WHERE – THEY DIDN'T TELL ME. IF YOU WANT TO FIND HIM – YOU MUST GET OUT OF THIS PLACE.

HOW MANY KIDS ARE OVER THERE? LOCKED UP?

I DON'T KNOW WHAT GOES ON – THERE ARE THE BOYS IN THE PRISON AND THEN THERE ARE THE *SPECIALS*.

SOMETHING CALLED THE *PSI PROJECT*. BUT I KNEW I HAD TO ACT WITH YOU BECAUSE OF THE TATTOO!

ALL RIGHT. THERE IS ONE THING – THERE'S A BOY IN THE BLOCK NAMED *DANIEL MCGUIRE*. HE'S COMING WITH ME.

HIS MOTHER HELPED ME. I *PROMISED* HER.

I'LL SEE WHAT I CAN DO. KORING WILL ARRIVE SOON. STAY HERE –

– I WILL COME FOR YOU WHEN IT GETS DARK.

THAT PROVES THIS IS REAL. HAVE I BEEN CAPTURED AGAIN?

NO — THIS IS TOO DIFFERENT. AND THESE BODIES... A WAR HAS TAKEN PLACE.

AND I'VE JUST WOKEN UP ON THE LOSING SIDE.

ALL MY LIFE'S BEEN COMPLETELY INSANE — READING MINDS, CHASED BY THE POLICE — I'VE LEARNED TO LIVE WITH THAT, SO WHY NOT THIS?

SOMEHOW... I'M IN ANOTHER PLACE. MAYBE EVEN ANOTHER PLANET!

IT'S LIKE ALL THOSE BATTLES I'VE SEEN IN THE MOVIES. ALL THESE DEAD MEN —

— BUT WHO WERE THEY FIGHTING? WHOEVER THEY WERE, THEY WERE UTTERLY RUTHLESS.

THEY LEFT NOBODY ALIVE.

EXCEPT FOR A MONK?

THANK GOD! MAYBE HE CAN TELL ME WHERE I AM, WHAT HAPPENED!

RAG DAGGER A MARRAD HAG!

HE'S NOT TOO FAR. WE WILL CAMP TONIGHT IN THE CITY OF CANALS.

THE CITY OF CANALS?

IT HAS NO OTHER NAME — IF IT HAD, IT WOULD HAVE BEEN LOST LONG AGO.

WE SHOULD LISTEN TO FINN. IF WE STAY HERE TALKING, WE'RE GOING TO END UP WITH OUR INNARDS ON A STICK.

I SUGGEST WE MOVE.

HERE — I'LL HELP YOU.

I'VE NEVER SAT ON A HORSE IN MY LIFE — CLOSEST WAS AT CLARK COUNTY FAIR...

HAH! I DON'T FEEL NERVOUS AT ALL — IT'S JUST LIKE IT WAS WITH THE SWORD!

TO THE CITY, THEN.

THAT SAID, NOBODY ELSE NEEDED TWO MEN TO HELP THEM UP.

DON'T **SAY** ANYTHING.

DON'T **DO** ANYTHING.

JUST PLAY YOUR PART. IT'S IMPORTANT.

SAPLING!

IT'S SAPLING...

HE'S **ALIVE!**

DO YOU BELIEVE ME NOW?

WE TOLD YOU THE TRUTH. HE'S HERE. WE FOUND HIM.

SAPLING!!!

FLINT IS MY TWIN? THEN HE'S *SCOTT*. I WAS LOOKING FOR HIM WHEN I WAS SHOT. THAT'S HOW I ENDED UP HERE.

I *HAVE* SEEN YOU BEFORE — BUT IT WASN'T REAL. IT WAS A DREAM.

PEOPLE USED TO THINK THAT DREAMS DIDN'T MEAN ANYTHING. BUT THERE'S A *DREAM WORLD* WE VISIT SOMETIMES.

THAT'S HOW WE FOUND OUT WHO WE WERE. THAT'S HOW WE FOUND EACH OTHER IN THE FIRST PLACE.

YOU SHOULD START AT THE BEGINNING. YOU'RE A ROTTEN STORYTELLER.

THERE *WAS* NO BEGINNING FOR ME — OR IF THERE WAS, I DON'T REMEMBER IT.

MATT'S THE ONLY ONE WHO KNOWS THE WHOLE TRUTH AND HE NEVER TELLS US ANYTHING!

START WITH THE *FIVE*.

ALL RIGHT! BUT DON'T INTERRUPT ME!

ADULTS TAKING SECOND PLACE TO CHILDREN —

THAT'S WHAT I *REALLY* CALL THE END OF THE WORLD!

I'VE ONLY BEEN ALIVE ABOUT FIFTEEN YEARS, AND THIS WAR HAS CONTINUED FOR MORE THAN *FIFTY*.

THAT'S WHY FOR ME, THERE NEVER WAS A BEGINNING. I WAS FAR AWAY, ON THE OTHER SIDE OF THE WORLD...

"HIS SOLDIERS DIED ALL AROUND HIM. SAPLING FOUGHT UNTIL THE END."

"THEY CUT HIM DOWN. HE TOOK THREE ARROWS IN HIS CHEST. AND THEN THEY CUT HIM TO PIECES, *LAUGHING* AS THEY DID IT."

THEY CUT OFF HIS HAIR AND HIS FINGERS FOR SOUVENIRS. THEY BUILT A FIRE AND *BURNED* THE REST.

JUST *TWO MEN* SURVIVED – SENT BACK TO TELL US WHAT HAPPENED. THE FORTRESS WAS EMPTY – SAPLING HAD DIED FOR NOTHING.

SO IT WAS ALL OVER.

THERE WOULD *NEVER* BE FIVE OF US. WE HAD LOST. I THOUGHT MATT HAD BETRAYED US. I *HATED* HIM.

BUT THEN HE CAME TO ME. HE TOLD ME TO RIDE THIS RUINED CITY, AND THEN GO TO SCATHACK HILL WITH FINN, ERIN AND CORIAN.

WE DID – AND THERE WE FOUND YOU. I CRIED BECAUSE I THOUGHT YOU WERE SAPLING.

ARE YOU? BECAUSE WE *NEED* YOU TO BE. TOMORROW WE FIGHT THE OLD ONES FOR THE LAST TIME.

THEY'RE WAITING FOR US, LESS THAN A LEAGUE AWAY. WE NEED YOU TO BE *ONE OF US*.

I'M JAMIE. I'M SORRY.

I WISH I *COULD* BE THE PERSON YOU WANT ME TO BE – BUT I DON'T THINK I AM.

THEN IT'S OVER.

SAPLING IS *DEAD* AND THE *OLD ONES* HAVE *WON*.

THE NEXT DAWN.

I'M JAMIE ... NOT SAPLING...

WHURGH!

YOU'RE AWAKE. DID YOU HAVE ANY DREAMS?

I WAS TOO TIRED FOR DREAMS.

LOOK – SAPLING – I'M NOT HIM. I KNOW YOU WANT ME TO BE, BUT I'M NOT.

MAYBE NOT – BUT TODAY YOU HAVE TO BE.

YOU LOOK LIKE HIM. YOU SOUND LIKE HIM. AND IF I DIDN'T KNOW FOR SURE THAT HE HAD BEEN KILLED, I'D SAY YOU WERE HIM.

WHAT YEAR IS THIS?

IT'S THE YEAR AFTER THE ONE BEFORE.

I'VE HEARD IT SAID THERE WERE NUMBERS ONCE BUT THAT WAS LONG AGO AND THEY'VE ALL BEEN FORGOTTEN.

THE OLD ONES. THEY'VE MADE LIFE PAINFUL AND MISERABLE – BUT AT LEAST THEY MADE IT SHORT.

COME WITH ME. I HAVE SOMETHING TO SHOW YOU.

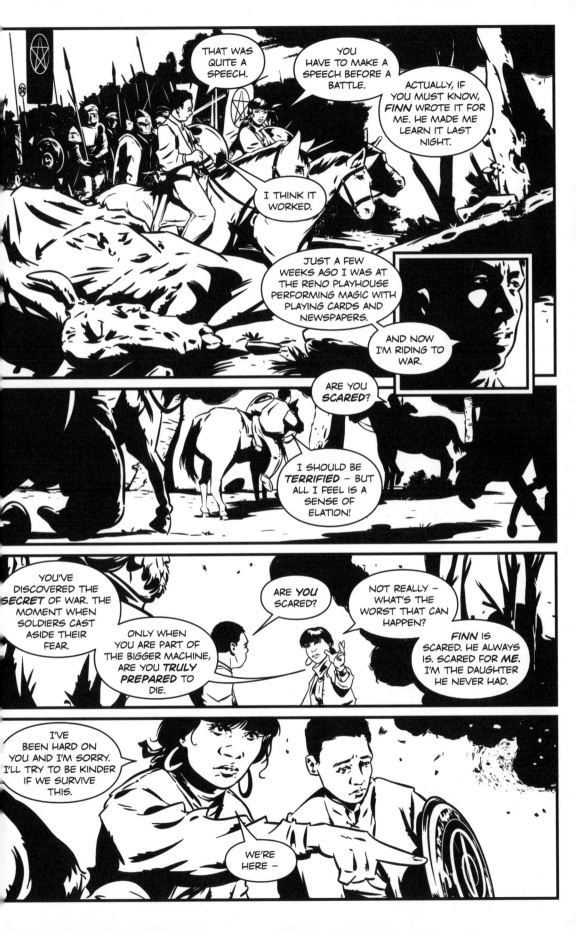

LOOSE ARROWS!!!

SKREEEEEEE!!!

I'M SORRY — BUT I HAVE TO **WAKE** YOU. WE HAVE TO TALK.

WHURGH?

SHOULD I LEAVE THIS? WHERE ARE WE GOING?

NO — BRING THE SWORD WITH YOU. IT'S NOT FAR.

THERE ARE THINGS I NEED TO **TELL** YOU BEFORE YOU GO. I CAN'T SPEAK OF YOUR WORLD — BUT THERE ARE WAYS I **CAN** HELP YOU.

YOU'VE TRAVELLED TO THE PAST — TWO CIVILIZATIONS SEPARATED BY TEN THOUSAND YEARS.

THE OLD ONES — THEY FEED ON **MISERY**. IT'S THEIR NATURE. THEY TORE APART ANYTHING THAT WAS BEAUTIFUL OR USEFUL.

THEY CHANGED THE ATMOSPHERE. THEY CUT DOWN FORESTS AND KILLED ALL THE ANIMALS. THEY POISONED THE RIVERS AND CLOGGED UP THE SEAS.

WE FOUND EACH OTHER THROUGH OUR DREAMS. THERE ARE THE TWO WORLDS, PAST AND FUTURE —

— BUT THERE IS A **THIRD**, A SORT OF TUNNEL BETWEEN THE TWO. IT HAS A GREAT SEA, AND AN ISLAND.

I DON'T KNOW **WHAT** SHE DID, BUT THIS MORNING SHE PACKED UP HER HORSE AND LEFT.

I FIGURED YOU WERE DEAD — I'M GLAD YOU'RE NOT!

I'LL LEAVE YOU TWO TOGETHER. I MUST PREPARE THE MEAL.

I'D LIKE TO GO HOME NOW. THERE'S NO CELL PHONE RECEPTION HERE — I HAVEN'T BEEN ABLE TO PHONE MY MOM.

CAN YOU TELL ME ABOUT **SILENT CREEK**?

THEY GRABBED ME ON MY WAY HOME FROM SCHOOL. THERE WERE **SIXTEEN** OF US IN THE BLOCK — FOUR GIRLS, THE REST WERE BOYS.

THEY DID THESE **EXPERIMENTS**. THEY WERE LOOKING FOR KIDS WI POWERS. THEY HAD A SPECI ROOM — THE ONLY PLACE I SILENT CREEK MY POWERS WOULD WORK.

THAT EXPLAINS WHY I COULDN'T FORCE KORING...

THEY WERE SEARCHING FOR THE **FIVE**.

THEY CALLED IT THE **PSI PROJECT**. THEY DID TESTS AND **HURT** US. THEN THEY LEFT US ALONE.

AFTER THAT WE WERE JUST KEPT IN PRISON. WHICH SUCKED, AS WE HADN'T DONE **ANYTHING** WRONG.

AND THEN **SCOTT** ARRIVED. HE HAD THE CELL NEXT TO MINE. THEY TOOK HIM AWAY AND MUST HAVE DONE A LOT OF **BAD THINGS** TO HIM BECAUSE HE STOPPED TALKING TO ANYONE.

THE BALD MAN — **BANES** — WORKED ON HIM. THEN THIS WOMAN ARRIVED, THIN AND SCRAWNY WITH GREY HAIR. EVERYONE WAS SCARED. I NEVER LEARNED HER NAME.

DANNY!

YOU BROUGHT HIM BACK. HOW CAN I THANK YOU?

WHAT ABOUT SCOTT?

SCOTT WASN'T THERE.

YOU'RE HURT!

I'LL BE ALL RIGHT.

DO YOU MIND IF I GO IN? I NEED TO LIE DOWN.

OF COURSE. YOU MUST TELL ME...

I'M SO SORRY –

– ABOUT SCOTT.

AUBURN, CALIFORNIA.

GET THE SENATOR DOWN!

SCOTT!

JAMIE TYLER? YOU DON'T KNOW ME — BUT I'M A FRIEND OF JOHN TRELAWNEY.

I'M *NATHALIE JOHNSON.* I'VE BEEN LOOKING FOR BOTH OF YOU. I CAN HELP YOU. WE HAVE TO GET YOU BOTH AWAY.

I *KNEW* I RECOGNIZED THAT KID. HE'S THE ONE FROM *NEVADA.*

CONTROL — I HAVE A *WANTED FELON* IN MY SIGHTS — *JAMIE TYLER.*

REQUEST ARMED BACKUP.

SCOTT! IT'S *JAMIE!* NIGHTRISE IS FINISHED — IT'S OVER! EVERYTHING'S GOING TO BE OK!

WHAT HAVE THEY *DONE* TO HIM?

WHAT HAVE THEY DONE?

JAMIE! SCOTT!

ARE YOU ALICIA MCGUIRE? I'M A *FRIEND.* JOHN TOLD ME ABOUT YOU.

WE CAN'T TALK HERE — WE NEED TO GET THESE BOYS ON THEIR WAY.

TYLER!

JAMIE TYLER, RIGHT?

NO. JAMIE TYLER *WAS* HERE, BUT HE'S *GONE.*

YOU MISSED HIM. AND NOW YOU HAVE TO HELP ALL THESE PEOPLE.

YOU'RE RIGHT. I'VE GOT TO HELP THESE PEOPLE.

STOP THE CAR...

STOP THE CAR! I KNOW THIS LAY BY!

IT'S WHERE SCOTT AND I WERE *FOUND!*

I REMEMBER DERRY, OUR SOCIAL WORKER, TELLING US ABOUT IT. DOWN THERE IS A SACRED CAVE — *DE'EK WADAPUSH* — IT TRANSLATES AS *CAVE ROCK.*

I THINK THIS IS *GOODBYE,* ALICIA.

THANK YOU FOR HELPING ME. THANK YOU FOR *EVERYTHING.*

YOU DID IT ALL, JAMIE. NOT *ME.*

HERE — TAKE THIS. IT'S ONLY A HUNDRED DOLLARS — BUT IT MAY HELP.

WHOOOOOOOO

GOODBY. DANNY.

– IT TOOK US TO *PERU*!

IT'S *THIRTY HOURS* TO NAZCA.

PEDRO'S THERE. HE'S A *HEALER*.

HE CAN *HEAL* YOU. HE'LL MAKE YOU BETTER.

WE'RE *HERE*, SCOTT. WE'RE HERE.

TAXI

JAMIE. AND SCOTT.

FOUR OF THE *FIVE* COME TOGETHER –

END OF BOOK THREE

ANTHONY HOROWITZ is one of the most popular contemporary children's writers. Both The Power of Five and Alex Rider are number one bestselling series enjoyed by millions of readers worldwide.

When Anthony launched the Alex Rider series in 2000, he created a phenomenon in children's books, spurring a new trend of junior spy books and inspiring thousands of previously reluctant readers. Hailed as a reading hero, Anthony has also won many major awards including The Bookseller Association/Nielsen Author of the Year Award, the Children's Book of the Year Award at the British Book Awards, and the Red House Children's Book Award. The first Alex Rider adventure, STORMBREAKER, was made into a blockbuster movie in 2006.

Anthony's other titles for Walker Books include the Diamond Brothers mysteries; GROOSHAM GRANGE and its sequel, RETURN TO GROOSHAM GRANGE; THE DEVIL AND HIS BOY, GRANNY, THE SWITCH, and a new collection of horror stories, MORE BLOODY HOROWITZ. Anthony also writes extensively for TV, with programmes including FOYLE'S WAR, MIDSOMER MURDERS, POIROT, and most recently COLLISION. He is married to television producer Jill Green and lives in London with his sons, Nicholas and Cassian, and their dog, Limpy.

You can find out more about Anthony and his books at:
www.anthonyhorowitz.com
www.alexrider.com
www.powerof5.co.uk

TONY LEE, who wrote the script for this book, has been a writer for over twenty years. He started his career mainly in games journalism, but in the early nineties moved into writing for radio, TV and magazines. Tony spent over ten years working as a feature and scriptwriter, for which he has won several awards.

In 2004 Tony turned his attention to comics writing and has since worked for a variety of publishers, including Marvel Comics, IDW Publishing, Markosia, Rebellion, Panini and Titan. He has contributed to many popular and high-profile properties such as X-MEN, DOCTOR WHO, SPIDER-MAN, STARSHIP TROOPERS, WALLACE & GROMIT and SHREK.

In 2008 Tony was nominated in the category for "Best Newcomer Writer" at the prestigious Eagle Awards.

With artist Dan Boultwood, Tony created THE PRINCE OF BAGHDAD, which was serialized in the David Fickling / Random House weekly children's comic THE DFC. He is the author of the highly-acclaimed graphic novels OUTLAW: THE LEGEND OF ROBIN HOOD and EXCALIBUR: THE LEGEND OF KING ARTHUR published by Walker Books.

www.tonylee.co.uk

NIGEL DOBBYN is a prolific comics artist for 2000AD including work on STRONTIUM DOGS – RETURN OF THE GRONK and THE DARKEST STAR by Garth Ennis and RED RAZORS by Mark Millar. He has contributed to three issues of JUDGE DREDD: LEGENDS OF THE LAW published by DC Comics as well as Fleetway's SONIC THE COMIC.

Nigel provides illustration, design and licensed character work for many different clients, as well as writing and drawing BILLY THE CAT for the Beano and colouring and lettering MACBETH and THE TEMPEST for Classical Comics.

NIGHTRISE: THE GRAPHIC NOVEL is Nigel's first graphic novel for Walker Books. He lives in Cleveland, UK.

First published 2014 by Walker Books Ltd
87 Vauxhall Walk, London SE11 5HJ

10 9 8 7 6 5 4 3 2 1

Text and illustrations © 2014 Walker Books Ltd

Based on the original novel *NightRise*
© 1986, 2007 Anthony Horowitz

Anthony Horowitz has asserted his moral rights.

This book has been typeset in CC Dave Gibbons

Printed and bound in Singapore

British Library Cataloguing in Publication Data:
a catalogue record for this book is available from the
British Library

ISBN 978-1-4063-1661-2

www.walker.co.uk

www.powerof5.co.uk